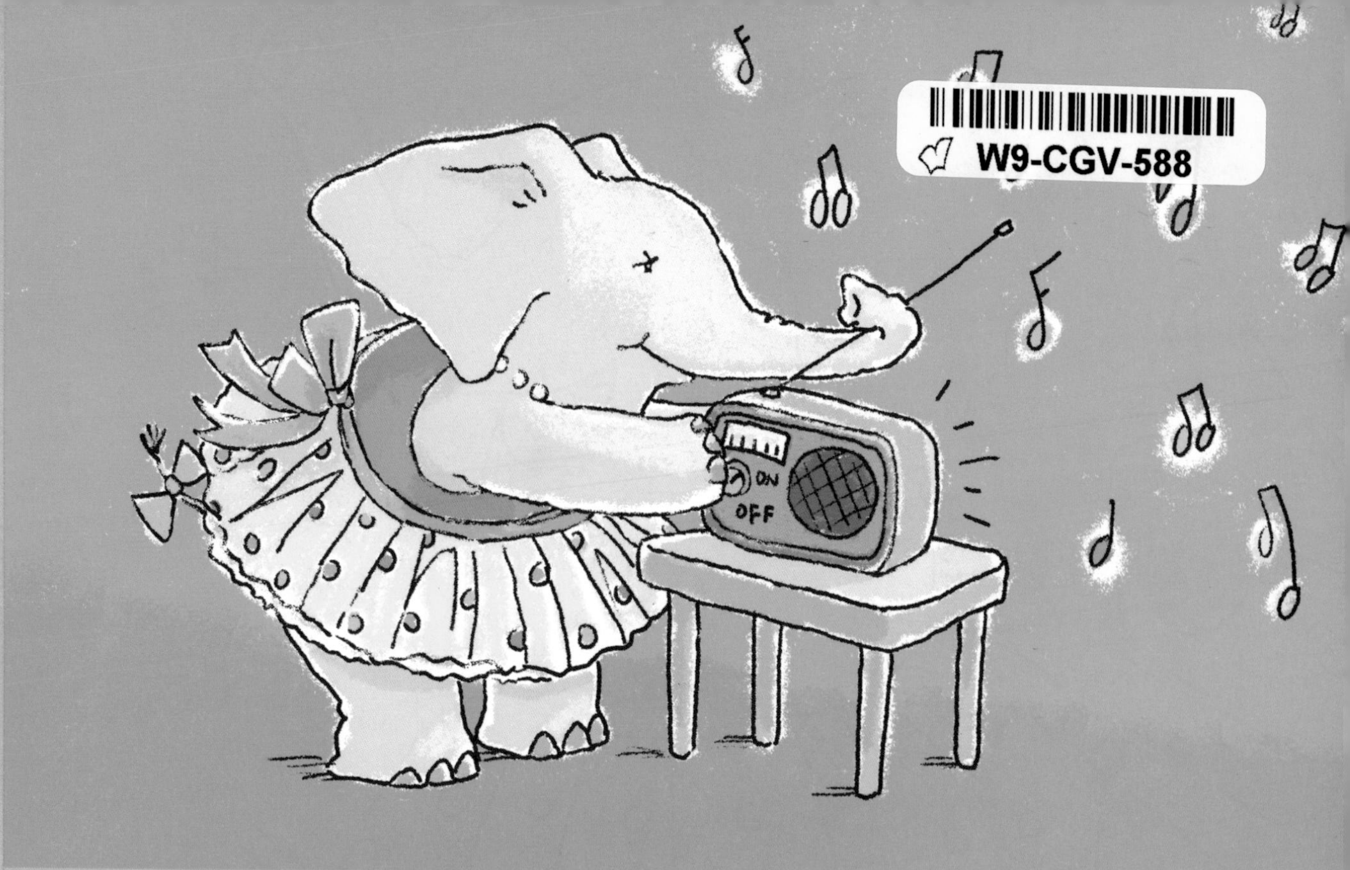

Edna turns on the radio.

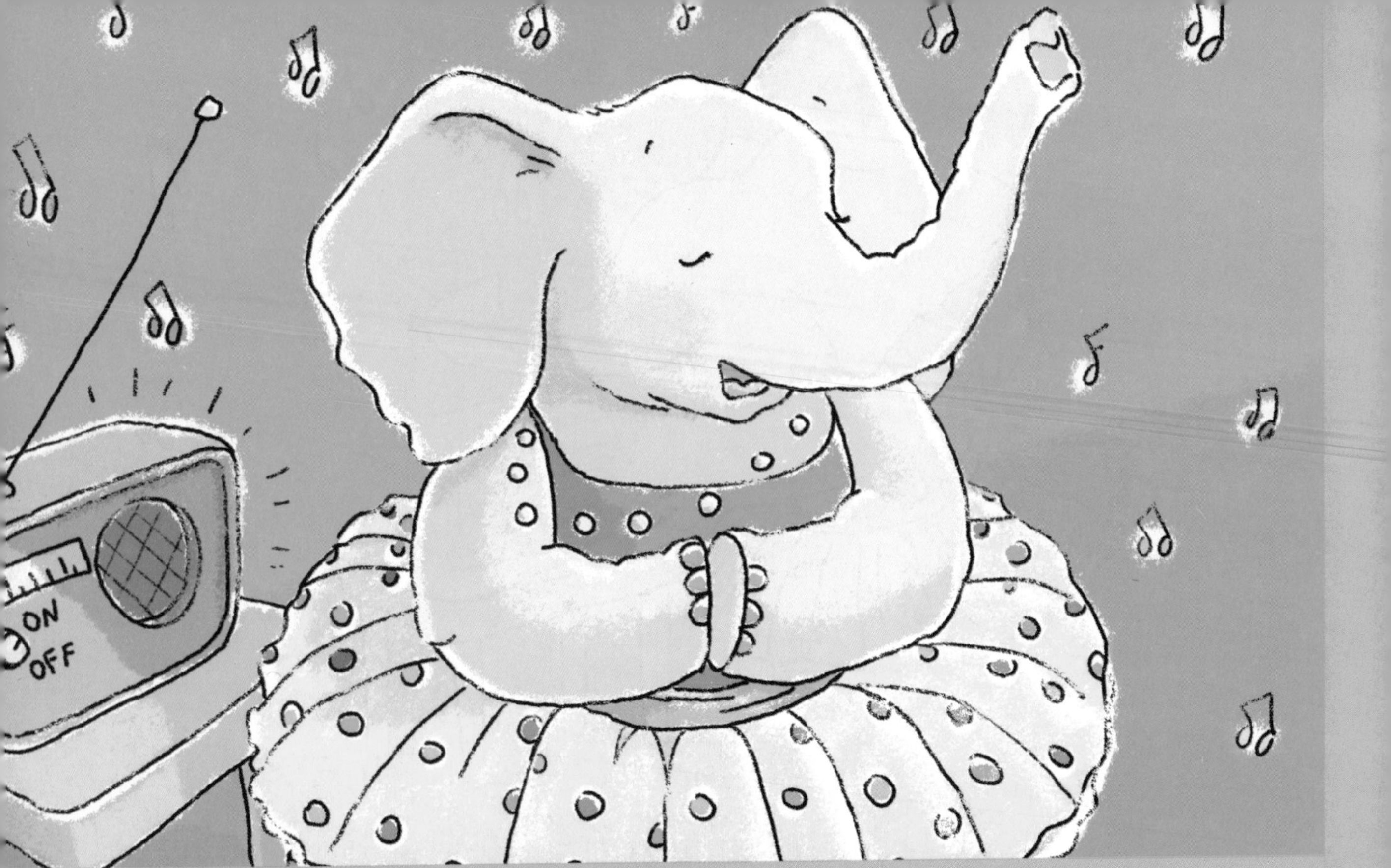

She sings.

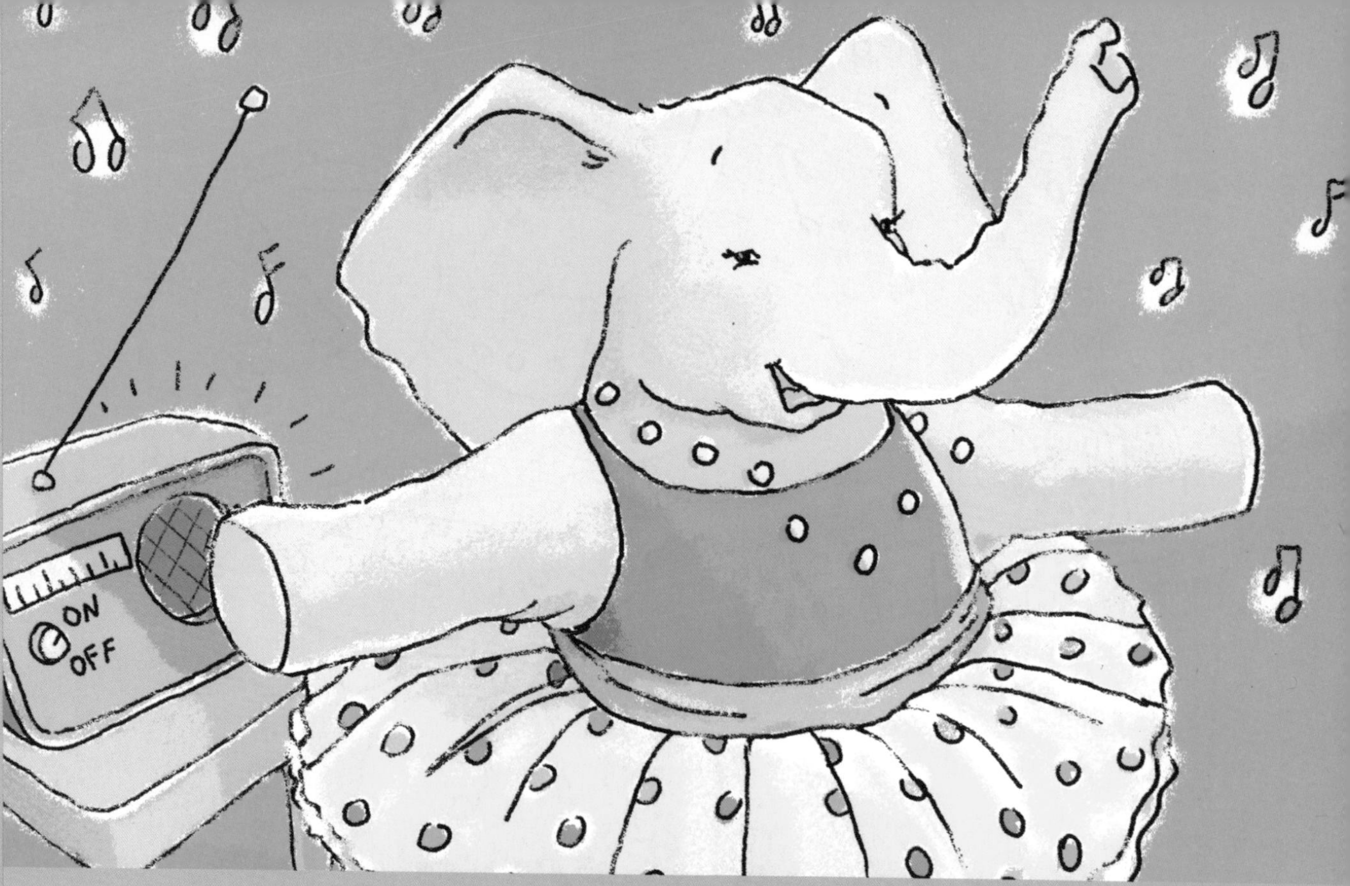

She opens her arms.

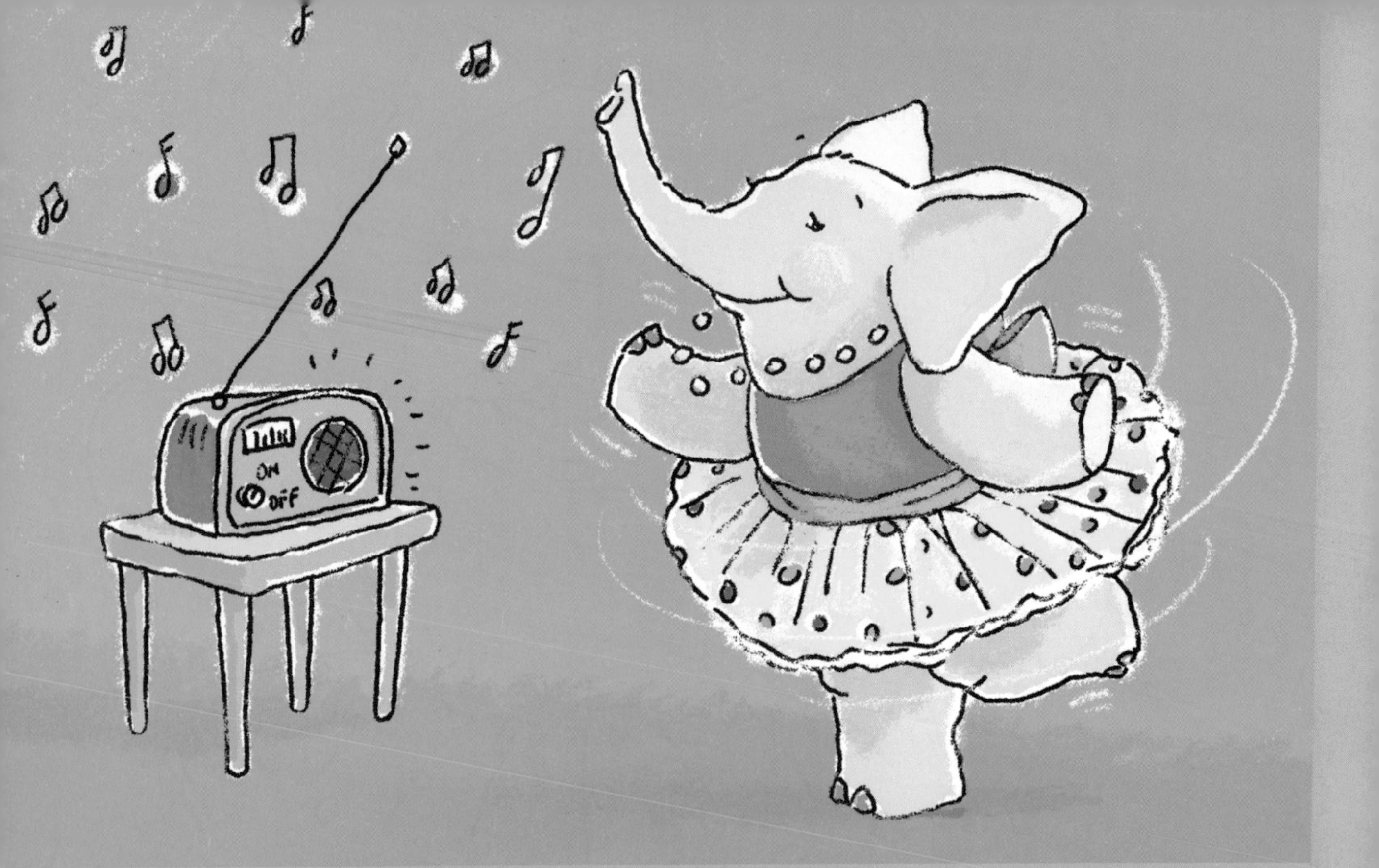

She stands on one foot.

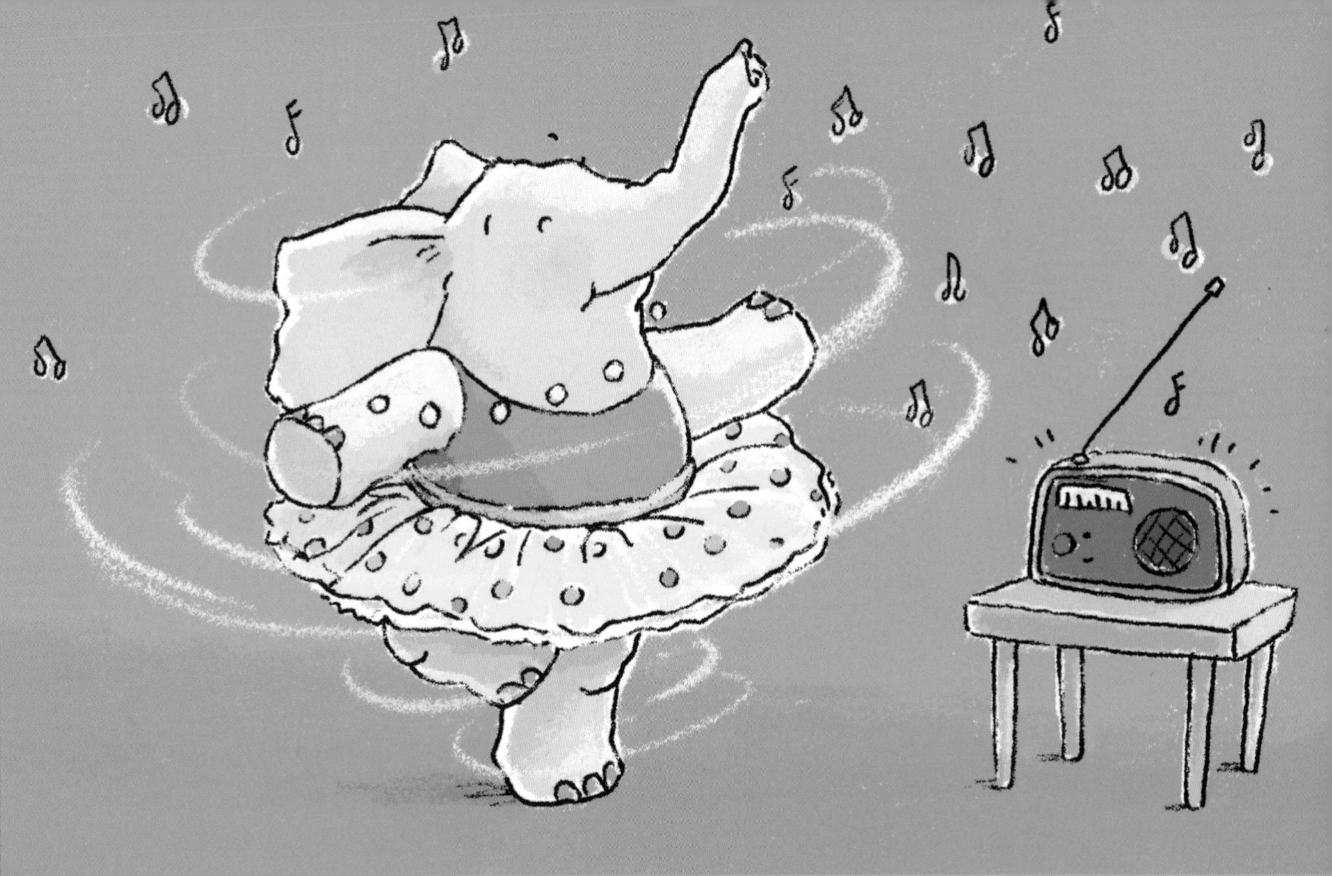

She spins.

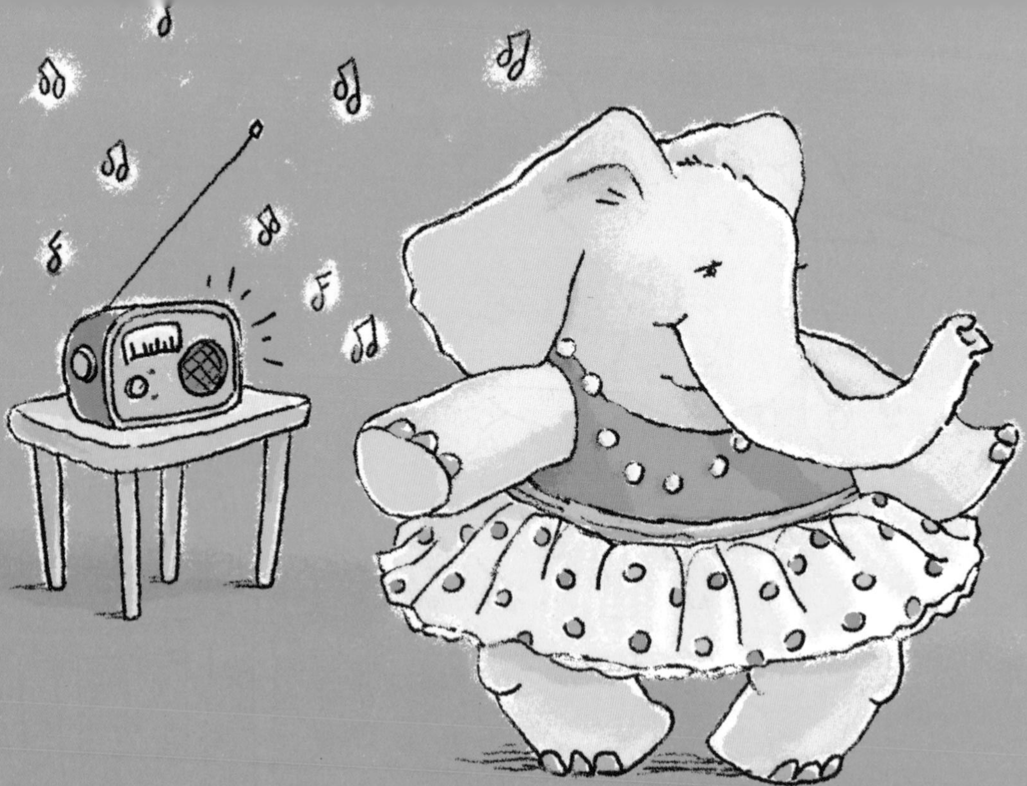

She bends her knees.

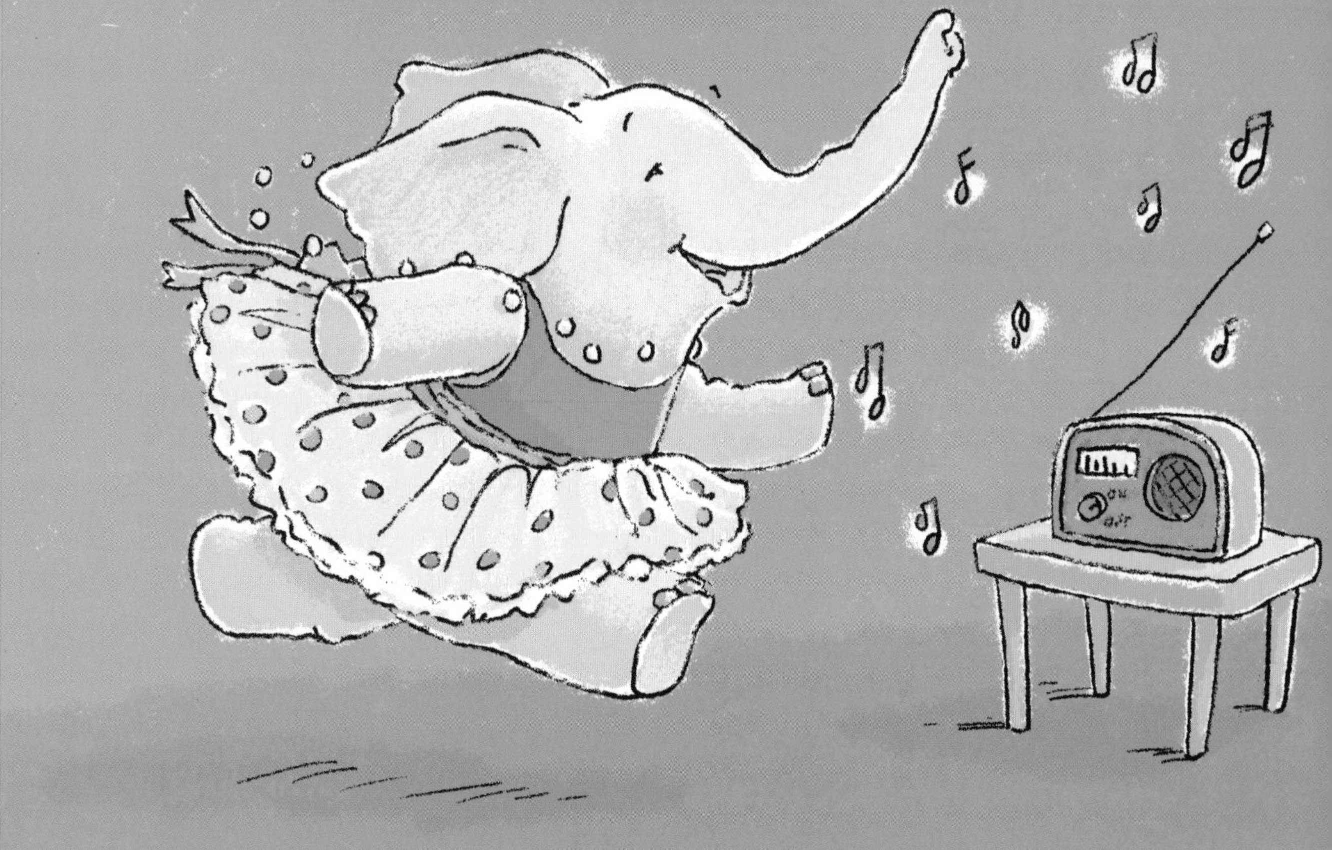

She leaps.

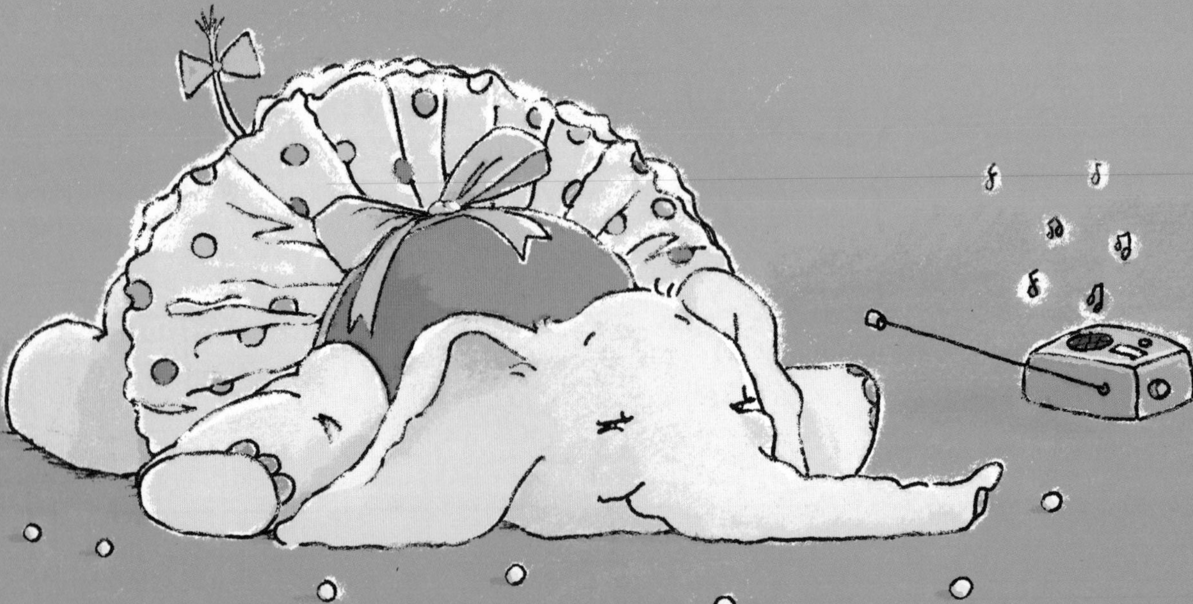

CRASH!